This Walker book
belongs to:

....

....

Text © 2013 Michael Rosen
Illustrations © 2013 Katharine McEwen

The right of Michael Rosen and Katharine McEwen to be identified as
author and illustrator respectively of this work has been asserted by
them in accordance with the Copyright, Designs and Patents Act 1988

This book has been typeset in Shannon Book, Kosmik, True Crimes

Printed in China

British Library Cataloguing in Publication Data: a catalogue record
for this book is available from the British Library

ISBN 978-1-4063-5550-5

www.walker.co.uk

SEND FOR A SUPERHERO!

WALKER BOOKS
AND SUBSIDIARIES
LONDON · BOSTON · SYDNEY · AUCKLAND

MICHAEL
ROSEN

KATHARINE
McEWEN

It was bedtime and Dad was reading
Emily and little Elmer a story.

It's bedtime and dad is reading a story:
'DANGER! THE TERRIBLE TWO ARE
TRYING TO DESTROY THE WORLD!'
Find out if one boy and a load of superheroes save the day.
– and if Emily and little Elmer
ever fall asleep.

SEND FOR A
SUPERHERO!

"Danger!" Dad began. "The Terrible Two are trying to destroy the world!"

"Who are the Terrible Two?" said Elmer.

"Look," said Dad, "there's Filth... He pours muck and slime over everything."

"And there's Vacuum," said Emily.

"He can suck money and jewels and treasure out of people's pockets, out of drawers, even out of banks," said Dad.

"Wow!" said Elmer.

"I'm nice," said little Elmer.

"No, you're not," said Emily.

"I am, aren't I, Dad?"
said Elmer.

"You're both very
good," said Dad.

Emily said, "Brad 40 knows what's going on, doesn't he, Dad?"

Little Elmer jumped up.

"I'm Brad 40!"

"No, you're not," said Emily.

"Heh-heh-heh-heh..."

"Enough cackling, thanks Dad," said Emily.

"Heh-heh-heh-heh-heh!" said little Elmer.

"No more cackling now, thanks Elmer," said Emily.

EXTREMELY BORING MAN...

YAWN

Walking is putting one foot in front of the other...

foot, then putting the other foot in front of the first foot...

Hooray for Boring Man! Zzzz

Then putti first ot

ZZZ

YAWN

Hooray! Zzz

Then putting the other foot...

...ARRIVED.

"And that," said Dad, "was how clever Brad 40 and Extremely Boring Man saved the world..."

Little Elmer and Emily lay in their beds sleeping soundly.

THE END

Dad crept out of the room.
Mum had been listening
at the door.
"Are they asleep?"
"Oh, yes,"
said Dad proudly.

"OH NO, WE'RE NOT!" shouted Emily
and little Elmer from the bedroom.

"WE TRICKED YOU!"

And so Dad started on a new chapter
of how Brad 40 saved the world.
Again.

Oh, no!

Michael Rosen's bestselling titles for children include **We're Going on a Bear Hunt, Little Rabbit Foo Foo, Michael Rosen's Sad Book, This Is Our House** and **Tiny Little Fly.** He has also written many collections of poetry, including **Bananas in My Ears.** Michael received the 1997 Eleanor Farjeon Award for distinguished services to children's literature, and from 2007 to 2009 was the Children's Laureate. Michael lives in London with his family.

Katharine McEwen has illustrated around forty children's books for all ages, including **Cows in the Kitchen** by June Crebbin, **My Dad, the Hero** by Stella Gurney, the Silver Street Farm series by Nicola Davies, the Sam's Science books by Kate Rowan and Jacqui Maynard, and Allan Ahlberg's Gaskitt stories. Katharine lives in Tonbridge, Kent.

Other books you might enjoy:

ISBN 978-1-4063-3097-7

ISBN 978-1-4063-2632-1

Available from all good booksellers

www.walker.co.uk